SPOOKY SPORTS DAY

By Erin Soderberg

Illustrated by Duendes del Sur

Hello Reader — Level 1

ISBN 0-439-31850-5

12 11 10 9 8 7   4 5 6 7/0

Cover Designed by Robin Camera/ Interior Designed by Maria Stasavage
Printed in the U.S.A.
First Scholastic printing, October 2002

SCHOLASTIC INC.

New York Toronto London Auckland Sydney
Mexico City New Delhi Hong Kong Buenos Aires

and his friends were at

the park.

 was excited to help their

friend Mrs. Holm with Lakeside

Elementary School sports day.

 , , and were in

charge of the toss and

tug-of-war.

 and were going to

help with snacks.

"Oh, no!" cried Mrs. Holm. "The and the are missing!"  tried to find the .

But all  found were

footprints and kids running

relays.

"Like, I hope a didn't take

the ," said 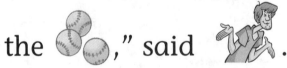.

"We better look for clues, gang,"

 said.

was scared, but he wanted

to run relays and play catch.

He knew he had to help find the

missing  and .

He hoped he wouldn't find a

.

 looked under a 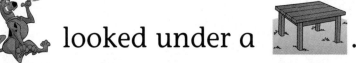.

He found a family of

carrying their lunch.

But he did not find the .

found  by the

cart.

"Hey, , did you find the

 or ?"  asked.

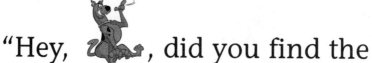 shook his head.

The 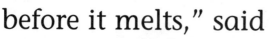 was very hot.

"Like, we better eat this

before it melts," said .

"Rokay!" said.

and looked in a

basket next to the  .

They found and .

But the were not there.

Neither was the .

They followed a .

But it did not know where the

 or the  were.

, 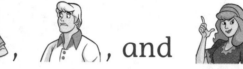 , and found

some kids from Mrs. Holm's

class tying their  .

"Did you find the ?" a

boy asked.

"We want to have the

toss!" said a girl.

"Let's keep looking, gang,"
 told  and .

A man was flying a .

"Have you seen a filled

with ?" asked him.

"Yes, I saw a at the top

of the this morning," the

man said.

"Let's check the  for

clues," said.

, , and ran to

the top of the .

They found and  on

the  .

But they did not find the

full of  .

"Ruh-roh!"  pointed at

some  .

"Like, I hope those aren't from

the !" said.

"Look," said . "They lead

down the to the

 !"

"We need to follow the

down to the ,"

said.

"Will you look in the if I

give you a ?"  asked

.

"Rokay!"  said.

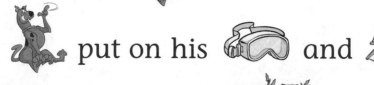 put on his and .

He dove into the .

found the full of

 in the .

"The must have rolled

down the  and into the

 ," said.

"There was no ," said .

"You saved sports day, !"

Mrs. Holm said.

"Scooby-Dooby-Doo!"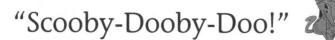

barked.

Did you spot all the picture clues in this Scooby-Doo mystery?

Each picture clue is on a flash card. Ask a grown-up to cut out the flash cards. Then try reading the words on the back of the cards. The pictures will be your clue.

Reading is fun with Scooby-Doo!

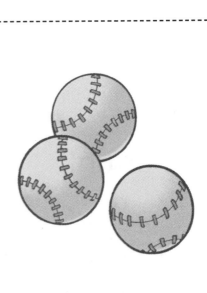

Scooby Snacks	Scooby-Doo
Fred	Daphne
softballs	Velma

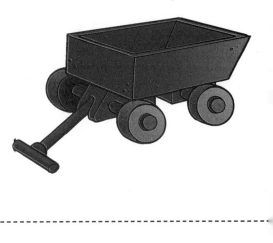

wagon	Shaggy
picnic table	monster
ice cream	ants

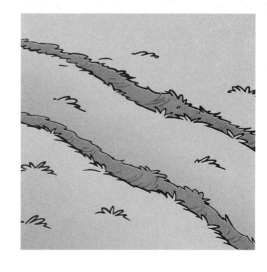

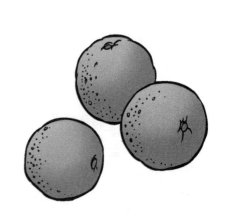

tracks	sun
oranges	swings
butterfly	potato chips

kite	shoes
swim mask	pond
hill	flippers